CW01497317

ASTRAEA

A List of the Female Convicts on board the Lady Penrhyn

Names	Age	Crimes	Trades	No of years transported
Francis Davis *Highwayman*	22	[Robbery]	Service	14
Ann Yates	19	House breaking	Milliner	7
Mary Love	60	Theft	Service	14
Ann Colepits	28	Privately Stealg	Do	17
Eliz Lock	23	Housebreakg	Do	17
Mary Gamble	37	Defraud	Do	7
Olivia Gascoine *coin*	24	Theft	Do	7
Mary Tilley	30	House breakg	Do	17
Sarah Davies	26	Shop Lifting	Glove maker	7
Ann Sincell	30	House breaking	Mantua maker	7
Mary Wilkes alias Turner	21	Privately Stealing	Service	17
Eliz Bird	15	Lamb Stealing	Do	17
Ann Dawley alias Twisfield	23	Highway robbery	Do	17
Sarah Bellamy	17	Privately Stealing	Do	17
Mary Davis	25	House breaking	Do	17
Mary Mitchell	19	Stealing	Do	17
Mary Boulton	29	Housebreakg	Do	17
Mary Dickenson	26	Barrow woman	Stealing	7
Amelia Levy	19	Shop lifting	Furrier	7
Eliz Hall	18	House Robbery	Service	7
Margarett Younes	45	Highway Robbery	Do	Life
Hannah Mullens	20	Robbery	Do	7
Eliz Packford	70	Shoplifting	Do	7
Eliz Innes alias Osborn	28	Robery	Do	14
Eliz Tuzby	22	House breakg	Do	7
Eliz Lee	24	Robery	Do	7
Mary Brenham	17	House breakg		7
Eliz Mipsley	28	Pick pocket	Needlework	Life
Ann Redd	22	Street Robery	Service	
Susannah Huffnell	24	Buying Stolen Goods	Do	7

National Library of Australia

ASTRAEA

Kate Kruimink

WEATHERGLASS BOOKS

For Ella, a woman of strength and kindness.

ASTRAEA

I

It was six o'clock in the morning and the ocean was pooled dark glass. The sky was nothing, but also nothing else, not cloud nor sun nor moon. There was a slow creak in the air.

The maybe-friend Sarah Ward had poisoned herself again in the night and was convulsing in the hospital below. The other women in the pen had made flocks of themselves, bonnets fluttering, all done up to their necks in their coarse greys and browns like common pigeons. Even that terrible old madwoman had found company. But without Sarah Ward, the girl sat alone.

'I give you a riddle! What is neither here nor there?' called the madwoman to the eye-rolling friends about her. 'What is trees where no trees grow? What is thirst in water?'

'No one wants riddles,' called back a tolerant young mother from a saner circle.

The three women dry-stoning the deck raced one another into the final corner, laughing, and stood to stretch their arms back and forth.

Somehow all the women had got the measure of each other already – had done it almost immediately, just by clapping eyes on one another – but the girl did not know anything about any of them really, aside from a few observances that, when put together, did not make a pattern she might begin to anticipate. She certainly did not know what to make of the maybe-friend Sarah Ward, who sat with her except on inscrutable occasions when she would sit away from her and not look at her and talk animatedly to some Northerner or Welshwoman or other instead, and who whispered filthy things hot into her ear that she thought the girl would need to know, and who lay restless beside her at night, annoying the other two women who shared their berth, and who gave the girl food from her own plate because she thought the girl had become too thin and colourless, and who kept hurting herself, rending her flesh and bringing her secret insides right out into the brisk sea air with such purpose she was like a fanatical monk offering utter bodily abjection up to God. But Sarah did not much care for God because He did not much care for her, because if He did she would be in her natural state, she said, which was of course a palace with fine eider-down quilts.

That doctor, that Scotsman, did not approve of any of them and especially he did not approve of Sarah. His disapproval had not yet cured her, but still he was trying it.

Someone began to sing 'The Bitter Withy'. The chaplain did not often allow singing above decks, lest it draw the sailors' attention, and when he did it was only hymns. He was forever creeping about, but now he stopped his creeping and straightened. The singing woman was Elizabeth Duncan, who was known to all because the captain often took her away from them for his own purposes, especially in the night. She was not the finest of the singers, not like Margaret Muir with the voice of cream and honey, but still it was pleasant to hear her. *Our Saviour asked his mother dear / If he might play at ball*, she sang, but the chaplain gave a cry and strode to her, incredulous. 'Jesus Christ did not play at ball,' he told her, voice trembling, neck all red.

11

Elizabeth stopped, biting her next word in half. 'But it is religious,' the girl heard her whisper as he stalked away.

The chaplain was very bad at religion. Worse than the women. The afternoon before, he had come down and read to them while their dinner got cold. He had done the reading that begins *Judge not, lest ye be judged*. It had a nice ring to it, but the effect of it was that all hundred or so women and girls closed their ears to him, because obviously they had already been judged, and therefore it followed that they now might judge freely. That was so evident they did not even need to discuss it afterwards. They simply exchanged intellectual glances over cold mutton.

A girl rose from a circle of other girls and staggered to the railing. She crouched and sat there with her arms wrapped around her middle. 'Mary, what are you about now?' called one of the others. She did not reply, but instead knelt and bent forward until her head was touching the deck. She started rifling through her skirt, hiking it up, scrabbling underneath, crying. The others giggled uneasily.

'Come now,' said a woman with a stern voice, rising and going to her. 'Stop that.'

But the girl only cried louder. 'It's out of me!' she said. 'It's hanging out of me!'

'What, girl?'

'I think it is my womb!' she cried, and sat heavily. 'Look!' She spread her knees and began to pull her skirts up.

The woman slapped them down. 'There are men about, Piper!' she hissed, and indeed the sailors beyond the railings of their pen had raised their chins.

'And we don't want to see that anyway,' called someone else.

Moaning, Piper pulled herself upright and staggered off towards the hatch. 'I am going to see the doctor…' she said.

The woman who had gone to her stood with her hands on hips, shaking her head at their general company. 'Mary Piper was too long in a dark cell, and has gone a little mad,' she said. 'She will not stop talking about her womb being pulled out of her.'

But where the girl had walked, there was a trail of poppy-red blood.

The terrible old madwoman heaved herself up. 'I will go with her,' she said, conversationally. 'Wombs are like elbows to me. Very ordinary.' She hobbled towards the hatch, but the chaplain, who had never shown so much personality in one morning, grabbed her arm tightly. His face was white and ungiving.

'Clean it, and then sit down in silence,' the chaplain said. 'I will not have this filth.'

It was cold, but not as cold as it had been. The sky was too much of nothing to hold birds, and there were none in the lacework of rope above them. 'We are beyond birds now,' said the old madwoman, who could read the girl's mind through her face.

What is trees where no trees grow? What is thirst in water? the girl thought. There had been another part to it, but she could not remember it. There was no point when the answer was so obvious.

The ocean had no underneath to it, not to the eye. It looked solid as a floor, like yet another surface that would require their cleaning. It gave the girl a sense of a great and dreary obligation, as if she must drop off the side of the ship and set out across this surface and keep slipping around on it, catching her ankles on the ridges and seams, trying to dry-stone it until she fell down and shrivelled into a husk for lack of water. There was a poem about that, she thought, precisely that, but her mother had been a governess and was therefore joyless and grey and with no heart for poetry, so the girl didn't know it beyond a few words and a suspicion that it might speak to her. Water, water, everywhere, were the words she knew, and that it was about being thirsty and unlucky. She did not want to be thinking of her mother. She needed to scrape her mind clean like a farrier scraping a horse's hoof, great pieces of filth and dead matter dropping away. It was not her mother's fault. She had done quite well with the girl. It was just that her mother was now a memory and the girl had decided that memory was not her business, unlike Sarah Ward, who would do nothing but dwell, which clearly did not do her any good. Water, water, the girl said to herself. Water, water, everywhere.

The children were quiet that morning. Their soft little heads were tucked into the bosoms and shoulders and laps of their mothers, letting women's talk dapple them like sun through leaves, there in that treeless place. The girl had a pang of wanting. It had occurred to her only recently that she did not belong amongst those soft little heads, that instead she was the bosom or the shoulder or lap, or ought to be.

Outside their pen the sun caught the bright buttons of the officers. Two of these men stood talking, squinting out to sea. Sailors made their repetitive

movements, the hoistings, packings, scrubbings, pass-
ings, the hands-over-hands. She accidentally caught
the eye of one of the ones who was always leering, and
she looked away quickly.

There were other women near her there in their
pen, but not with her. She had put herself by the
bedding they brought up each morning to air, which
did not air well, because they were compelled to stack
the mattresses and fold the blankets. It was stinking,
and an unpopular place to sit. The woman from Cork
who did not like her was also near her and had set
her shoulders in such a way as to communicate this
dislike. She hated Sarah Ward, too, which was a great
comfort to the girl. Sarah Ward got terrible headaches
because of something the woman had done to her.

The woman from Cork did not like the girl because
she, the girl, had the Irish name of Maginn but was
in fact English not Irish, and yes her father was Irish
but she didn't even know the name of the place where
he had come from. He was a physician too, like the
Scottish doctor who was there with them to make sure
none of them was ill in the incorrect way. The Scottish
doctor's cures seemed harmful, and they certainly
hurt, but it was the correct kind of hurting. Sarah
Ward did the wrong kind.

Water, water, she thought. Water, water. Water, water, everywhere. Water and no more. Scrape the mind clean. If you are looking for freedom, this oblivion is the freedom that is available to you. And you probably ought to take what you can get.

The young sailor, not the one who leered all the time but the tall one with the easy way about him and the large hands and dark hair, came and found reason to pass into their pen and lean almost over her, tugging at something or other past her head. 'Ah, get away!' said a woman, and the chaplain paced over to watch the sailor go back to his business. The young sailor had found occasion at other times to be near her, too, and sometimes had whispered a thing or two, simple things made illicit, like that he was from Cornwall and his name was Peter Rowe, and that he would like to know also where she was from and what her name was.

A cry came muted from below, soaking upwards through decks and beams to prickle the back of the girl's neck, but the only other person who gave any sign of having noticed it was the terrible old mad-woman, for she turned her head in that moment.

Sarah Ward was seventeen. She said that they both ought to say they were twenty-one. The girl did not think she could pass for twenty-one. It was really very old. She was fifteen in body, but truly, as a person, she was far younger even than that. She was quite new.

||

A name is a kind of magic so strong that one or two hundred years ago you might have been hanged as a witch if you misused it, and one or two thousand years ago you wouldn't have been hanged but turned into a tree or something. Girls were forever being turned into trees back then. The name designates the thing, and without the name the thing is impossible to hold in the mind. It shifts and disperses its particles into the air. And if you give the thing a new name, then it dies and is reconceived right in the instant of renaming, snuffed out and then poured into the world again with a new idea attached to what it might be. In any case, that is what had happened to the girl. She was not a tree, but she had been transformed, had been killed in fact, killed by a tired clerk and reborn right back into the same body in one instant. There was a mistake with her name when it was being written down, and the mistake was that the clerk did not believe her when she said it, because it was too fanciful, too French. So he wrote down Maryanne instead, because that was more fitting, he said.

And so that was that: he killed the girl she had been, and when he finished writing her into being, there she was before him where he sat with his lips all pursed, this fresh new creature without a sully or a mark who was called Maryanne Maginn. And was she not glad to have been given, now, at the ripe age of fifteen, an ordinary name that belonged to other women and girls too, probably hundreds upon hundreds of them, a crowd into which she could scurry and hide? And if memories from before she was killed and reborn imposed themselves upon her, she was perfectly entitled to say to herself, *Well, that dark thing occurred to someone else, someone with a different name who is now dead, a name disapproved of, a name shamed, and not I. I am Maryanne Maginn, and the memories I have I may make anew.* And if her body remembered the dark things that had happened to the dead girl with the French name by, for example, leaking milk from its breasts and settling a peculiar aching into its own arms – well, that had nothing to do with her.

'Rouse yourself!' snapped the woman from Cork, who did not like her. The girl who had been named Maryanne was already awake, but still she had nearly missed the call down to breakfast. There would be a pint of cocoa and endless dry biscuit, endless as the sea itself. She would maybe try and take some to Sarah Ward in the hospital if she got up the courage.

She crept down amongst the others in the way they had all learnt to walk, a little like riding a horse, bracing and swaying with the up and down and side to side of it. They went down the ladder one by one, then through the grated door into the long, low room. It always felt cluttered below, though they kept it clean and tidy. It was busy with their tables and benches down the middle, separated one from the next by rough pillars thick as trees, and their berths stacked two high all along both bulkheads, and the door to the hospital at the far end, from which came groans day and night. There was light in the daytime, for the hatches above were left open, but when the sun set it was black as the grave. They were not allowed a flame.

Each table sat eight women and she found a corner

by a pillar with some women who did not mind her. Here she might mouse away her portion of cocoa and biscuit brought by the women whose turn it was to do the food, she thought. But then that terrible old madwoman who babbled and giggled and pulled at her hair quite deliberately sat beside her, her yellow stench clouding over them both.

'You're called Maryanne, are you not?' asked the old woman. They had been cleaners together the previous week, the two of them and a few others, responsible until Sunday for cleaning up the night vomit because they were never ill themselves. There was less to clean now, for everyone but one woman whose name the girl did not know had grown accustomed to the drop and pull of the ship. The woman who was still ill might die, they were saying, for she could barely keep water down, and she had been moved from rolling about in her berth with her vomit slopping over her and her berthmates to trembling in one of the real beds bolted down in the hospital with a pail beside her that she did not know how to aim for.

The old woman knew already that the girl's name was Maryanne. Anyway, it was hardly worth asking, even if she had forgotten. It was provoking.

'Yes, I am,' said the girl.

'Your bodice is wet,' said the old woman, and Maryanne pressed her hands against her chest and yes, it was flowered with two warm and milky stains blooming into the crust of old ones again. 'Wet wet wet,' said the old woman. 'Perhaps one of the mothers will die and you may have her baby, for you have misplaced your own. I know. I know the imps took it away!' she said, wagging her finger. Maryanne sat there with her hands flat against herself and looked wildly around, not at the women but anywhere else – the bulkheads, the table, the big pint cups going up and down in the women's fists, the flat pieces of sky and ocean outside the squares of light above.

'Oh leave her be, Mary Christie,' said an Irishwoman. This woman had a tired air, with great green eyes and black-and-grey hair soft at her temples. She untied herself at her back and unwrapped her shoulders and passed a brown shawl over the old Englishwoman to Maryanne. 'Wrap that about yourself, little girl, and do not mind Mrs Christie,' she said, and Maryanne did; she covered herself with the shawl and tried to not mind. Everything was salty and wrong, but then she told herself that it was nothing to do with Maryanne Maginn if her body leaked strange things at inopportune times, and that she could not possibly know what that meant because it belonged to someone who had been killed by a magical clerk. She returned to her breakfast and swallowed and swallowed and swallowed. And when the kind Irishwoman said, 'It will pass soon, dear. It will all dry up, don't you worry,' it did not even have anything to do with her at all, and so she smiled politely and remarked on the weather, which was in fact completely unremarkable and therefore as perfect as anything might possibly be outside Heaven to talk about. The shawl around her shoulders still smelt of the sheep which grew the wool.

'It sends some mad, you know,' said the Irishwoman, after a pause.

'The weather?' asked Maryanne.

'No, girl,' she said. 'Not the weather.'

'*I* am mad, Mrs Beattie,' said the terrible old woman, baring her teeth or what remained of them. '*I* have been sent mad by the devil, for I am a witch.'

'No you're not,' said the Irishwoman Beattie.

'Perhaps I am and perhaps I am not,' said Mary Christie. 'In the old days they would hang you or set fire to you for being a witch. Put screws on your fingers and pokers up you and rack you and kill you badly even if you said you wasn't one, even if you denied it. But now we're all enlightened, what they punish you for is saying you *are* a witch when really you ain't one. So either I really am one, or I am a criminal,' she said, and the women smiled despite themselves, there in their prison.

'You're putting it on so we'll all think you interesting and so the doctor will give you laudanum and tuck you up in one of those nice beds he has. But he isn't watching now and we're all tired of your antics, and this young girl has done nothing to you, so please you be quiet,' said the Irishwoman Beattie, but she was smiling too.

'Oh well,' said Mrs Christie.

'We must all pass the time somehow,' said the Irishwoman. The light brightened her bonnet. 'And I'm not Mrs Beattie, for I never married.'

Mrs Christie snorted. 'I cannot call you Miss. It is too terrible to be a miss with grey in your hair.'

'I do not ask you to! My name is Joan. And you do well know this.'

Mrs Christie shook her head and turned her attention back to Maryanne. 'Will you give me your wine at dinner time?' she asked the girl. 'They have stopped my ration. Perhaps I ought to ask that hussy Elizabeth Duncan if she might whisper a word about it into the captain's ear.'

'Mrs Christie, if you please!' said the kind Irishwoman, Joan Beattie, and Mrs Christie did then indeed quiet down to her cocoa. 'And don't use such words for poor Betsy Duncan. It is hardly her fault what happens.'

The chaplain was slouching about behind them, watching. The mothers were soaking dry biscuit in cocoa and feeding their children from their own fingers. One woman was undoing her bodice to suckle her baby, her older child of perhaps two or three leaning his head against her side, and milk was dripping from her and Joan Beattie was saying, 'Lydia, really, why do you let yourself get all filled up to the point of bursting like this? Just feed the babe when she is hungry.' The chaplain let out a huff and turned his back.

'I do not wish to give those men up there any reason at all to think of me,' said the woman. 'I can wait until we are below, and so can the baby.' She glanced irritatedly at a pair of young women whose voices had risen in their excitement at discovering they had once lived in the same street in Belfast. By them a slim little person was weeping softly, slowly unpinning her bonnet from her brown hair. The woman beside her, who Maryanne knew to be a gentle young countrywoman from Suffolk with three rosy children, began to stroke that brown hair. Maryanne thought, if only I could be unhappy in that manner, perhaps it would be better.

III

That Scottish doctor who disapproved was a mushroomy man, with a round white head and puffs of
grey hair each side, a big circle of a nose and a pair of
cool pale eyes.

'No, you may not bring her cocoa, young woman,'
the doctor said to Maryanne, standing there at the
door to the little hospital, holding the pint cup, and
she knew she had been wrong to try courage.

'Go and take it away,' he said, and there came
a sickly swell that made them both plant their feet
and brace, and the ship dropped in the sea and Sarah
Ward off behind him moaned and retched under the
shifting light. Maryanne held the cup of cocoa steady.

'Take it away and come back with a bucket of water
and a brush,' he said.

The hospital was not a bad place, although it smelt badly. It adjoined their sleeping and eating place but its shape was triangular, because it was situated at either the very front or the very end of the ship. She did not know which, because she grew disorientated below decks. It was small, but light. It had real square windows done in little grids and, besides these, a large lantern swaying on a chain which the doctor might light as he pleased. There was also a hatch above. This was for the use of the doctor and officers only, but was left open to the sun and air on fine, calm days. There were six beds, with spindly legs bolted to the decking. There was a folding screen set around the bed farthest to the left, but Maryanne could see a pair of bare feet twisted in the blanket beyond it.

As Maryanne knelt by her maybe-friend's bed and got up the vomit from down between the boards as best she could, employing brush and water and fingernails, she thought it might be good to become a little sick, and that maybe that was why Sarah Ward did it. She looked up at her, but all she could see was a hank of red hair off the side of the bed and a white hand dangling. She touched the fingertips and started, because on the forearm was a great round blister, larger than any she had seen, tight and round like a dewdrop seen from the perspective of an ant. But then she felt the doctor watching her and so she got back her task. If she took her time at it, she would not need to go back up and out amongst the women for a while. There was someone lumped up under the covers in another of the beds too, and a fourth bed was taken by the woman who never stopped being ill and might die, and Maryanne hoped that either person or the girl with the womb trouble behind the screen might be messily ill as well. But they were lying still.

'That will do, Maginn,' said the doctor, and so she went up on her heels and then stood. She did not know he knew her name. The doctor was looking at her there, looking with a critical eye. 'How old are you?' he asked, and when she said she was fifteen, Sarah Ward, sick but listening, gave a moan of despair that she had not said she was twenty-one as they had agreed. But I did not agree, Maryanne wanted to say, and anyway, the doctor will have it all written down, and can check, and we will get thrown in the coal-hole for lying.

'You speak well,' said the doctor.

'Thank you, sir,' she whispered.

'Have you an education?'

'Somewhat, yes, sir.'

'In order to do something towards defeating the idleness that so pervades your ranks, I have decided to employ some of the women who are educated to a degree as governesses, so the others might at least read their Bibles, and although you are so young and meek they would mostly tear you into pieces, perhaps you can assist,' he was saying to her, but she had stopped listening, because the mention of governesses made her think of her mother, or at least the mother of the girl with the French name, and so all she could think of then was, again: Water, water. Water, water, water, water, everywhere, water.

'Are you stupid?' asked the doctor, mildly enough.

'I don't know, sir,' she said, which was probably a stupid answer, and next, perhaps even stupider, standing there with vomit under her fingernails, the girl asked the doctor for a favour. 'May I sit with Sarah Ward?' she asked.

He was so surprised he told her he had a daughter her age, then he told her she must get rid of the slop in the bucket. And then he lectured her for some time about Edinburgh, which he said was a desirable place to live, with a fine old castle and rather a milder climate than many might expect. And then he complained a while that it was most inappropriate that he had no nurse to assist him. And then he told her that Sarah Ward was a wicked girl and she, Maryanne, ought to talk to her about God and the Angels and at the same time close her ears to anything Sarah Ward might contribute to the discourse. And in fact, at another time she ought to borrow a Bible and read it aloud to her. Old Testament. And finally he told her yes, very well, she might return after she had disposed of the foul water, if she had no other duties awaiting her and if she had washed her hands with soap, including under the fingernails, which seemed overly fastidious to her but something she could do regardless.

Sarah Ward expressed her sadness in such terrible ways that Maryanne could not even speak when she returned from disposing of the water, could do nothing but put a hand against Sarah's wet forehead and sit on the little stool beside her, tightening her body against the swell. The doctor was gone, so she did not have to talk about God and the Angels.

'Oh, Sarah,' said Maryanne. 'Why do you hurt yourself?'

'Tell me a story,' said Sarah Ward, her voice like catgut, her face bone-white and annoyed. 'If you're so educated.'

'I am not so educated. Sarah, how did you make this terrible blister?' she said, peering again at the straining blister on her forearm.

Sarah Ward frowned. 'Don't you know nothing? Don't you know medicine when you see it?' she asked. 'It's his doing. Look,' she said, and pulled her shift down to show Maryanne another great blister upon her chest, between her breasts, and showed her other arm with the same. 'My legs, too,' she said. 'It does burn when he puts them on, but I don't mind a little burning. He's drawing out – well, I don't know what exactly. Something bad. Now tell me a story.'

Maryanne stared, then collected herself. 'I do not know any stories at all.'

'Oh yes you do. Tell me about something.'

'Sarah,' said Maryanne again. 'Did one of the sailors get at you? Are you – you know—'

'You're a silly girl,' Sarah said, but her cracked mouth was wry. 'No, a sailor hasn't *got* at me yet. There's one I wouldn't mind, you know. It's that tall one with the brown skin. I think he's from Devon.'

'He is from Cornwall,' said Maryanne, and Sarah looked sharp.

'How do you know?' she asked, and Maryanne could not find the words to say that he had told her but that she had not invited the telling. 'I didn't know I had a little rival,' said Sarah at last.

'I should rather hang myself,' said Maryanne, quick and hot. 'Truly, I should rather die.'

'So should we all, I spose,' said Sarah, watching her. 'I'm tired of speaking now. Tell me a story to make it up to me.'

Maryanne put her hands slowly over her face and held them there briefly, breathing in the fat from the soap she had used. 'There was once a family,' she said, and Sarah Ward told her to speak up and take her hands off her face. 'There was once a family with a cook,' Maryanne said again, folding her hands in her lap, 'and the cook made them rice pudding for their supper. The next day, the girl of the family was playing in the garden when she saw a snake. The cook was also in the garden, picking apples for apple dumplings, and when she heard the girl scream, she dropped the apples everywhere and ran over lolloping like a great hound and took up the snake by its tail and whipped it against the wall until it was dead. Then she took it inside with the girl and cut open the belly of the snake and found inside a little brown mouse. And so they cut open the little brown mouse, and inside the mouse's belly were a few grains of rice pudding.'

'What?' said Sarah.

But the lump in the second bed said, 'Yes, very good,' and she rolled onto her back, long dark plait unweaving from the covers, profile fine in the warm light, and began to regale them. 'The thing that is truly comforting about a story is that it possesses deliberate meaning,' she said, in a voice most refined. 'It has a nice little moral, or is an allegory, or, at the least, is *about* something. This is not so in life, which of course has no meaning. One cannot, for example, think of one's home and the last time that one saw it, or any of the times before that, and understand it all, and how it is complete, and thus have done. As it is, Maginn has told us a nice little story, which stands as an entire world unto itself. We have the apple tree and the snake and the girl in the garden. Quite classically done, my dear, and we yawn our way contentedly through all such symbols and are satisfied by the end where the rice pudding in the mouse reminds us of the beginning of the story and so makes a circle. But if the story were not a story but a moment in a life, then it would not have ended there. The carcases of the snake and mouse would have had to be done away with, burnt, perhaps, or buried, and meanwhile there would be happenings upstairs and in the laneway and in the neighbours' houses and also in Egypt and so on and then perhaps someone – girl or cook – would have been scolded, and after that the cook would have made her apple dumplings, and the family eaten them, and so on and on, for years, for all of time, in fact. Do you see? Meaningless.'

Sarah Ward scoffed. 'All right, Lady Muck,' she said.

In the third bed, the woman who was always ill remained motionless, nothing but dank brown curls visible above the blanket.

'Has he asked you to be a governess yet?' Maryanne asked Lady Muck, but then Sarah Ward beside her winced and under the covers brought her knees up against her belly as the last of the colour went from her face.

'Maryanne—'

'I am here,' Maryanne said, leaning in, and tried to stroke her hair as she had seen that gentle young woman from Suffolk do, but the red hair felt dense and unyielding and she took her hand away again.

Sarah shuddered, head to toe, and gave a sharp groan. 'You smell of sour milk,' she whispered, eyes closed.

'I presume you are the girl in the story?' asked

Lady Muck, languid, but Maryanne was saved from responding by the doctor's return.

'Out, Maginn!' the man cried, shouldering the door open, carrying something in, a woman coming after him. It was the woman who also had all the milk coming out of her who had not wanted the sailors to see, and she had her hands up over her bonnet and brought them down to press at her breast. Maryanne stood. The woman did not have either her baby or her little boy with her.

'Sir, doctor, Sarah Ward has taken a turn...' she said.

'Out!' the doctor shouted at her again. 'Out! Out!' And he brought the parcel he was carrying over to the bed beside Sarah Ward's and from it unwrapped the woman's baby. The mother was beginning to say some words in a high and strangled voice. Maryanne looked again at Sarah Ward, curled into herself, her face into the pillow. Maryanne's breasts prickled with milk of her own once more, and her arms began their ache.

'And you – Piper – out with you too. There is no need for you to be lying there.' The bare feet behind the screen were pulled out of sight, and the doctor left the baby and went to push the screen to the side. It thumped and fell against a bulkhead. 'Get dressed and go out,' he said. 'I have done all I can for you.' The girl, Mary Piper, hunched and white, rolled off the bed and began to pick at her stockings lying by her boots on the deck.

'Woman! You – Fernsby! Fetch me the cantharides powder, quickly now,' said the doctor, over his shoulder, to the woman in bed who had ideas about life. 'It is in the drawer, there. In the cabinet.'

'I can fetch it,' said Maryanne, lingering by Sarah Ward's bed, but no one minded her. The mother was saying no, no, no blisters, you will burn her, and no one minded her either.

'You had better go,' said Lady Muck, whose name was Fernsby, sitting up, elegant, calm, her dark plait over her shoulder, swinging her stocking feet off the side of her bed. 'I shall attend this matter.'

'I do not wish to leave Sarah Ward,' Maryanne said, but Fernsby waved her off.

'There is nothing you might do for her,' she said. 'You are in the way.'

And so there was nothing else for Maryanne to do but go, though she took with her the image of Sarah Ward and her red hair wedged into the muscle of her heart. The girl with the womb trouble limped after.

.　　.　　.

In the place where they ate and slept there were some women standing together, talking in low voices, and they looked up at her when she came in. 'Did you see anything? What's happening?' asked one.

'I do not know,' said Maryanne, looking around for the girl with the womb trouble, but she hobbled past and through the open barred door and set herself to clambering painfully up the ladder. 'He said blistering for the baby.'

'Well, she mustn't allow that,' said one of the women. 'That's a dreadful thing to do to a child.'

'Blistering cured me of my cough,' said Joan Beattie.

'But you ain't a new baby, Joan,' replied the other.

'That is true. A baby's skin is so very fine,' said Joan, rubbing the tips of her fingers together as if testing the quality of silk. 'It did burn,' she added.

The skirt of one of the women was bunched. 'Come now,' that woman said, bending down and lifting a small child from behind her. The child held tightly to the rough fabric and the others had to gently pull it from his hands and smooth it down. 'Mama will return soon,' the woman said to the boy. And then, to Maryanne, 'How was Lydia?'

Maryanne hesitated, but then asked, 'Who is Lydia?' and the woman tutted.

'Why, the mother, of course! The mother of the baby and this wee lad.'

'She was upset,' said Maryanne. 'I think she said no blisters for the baby.'

The women nodded. 'Yes, you see? That's what I would say too,' said one.

The chaplain's legs and backside appeared beyond the doorway as he gingerly picked his way down. The woman with the child checked her skirt, checked the others had smoothed it down properly and no under-things were showing. The chaplain ducked in through the low door.

'What news?' the chaplain said. 'They tell me the Sculthorpe infant has taken ill?'

'Yes, sir. She knows,' said the woman holding the child, indicating Maryanne.

The chaplain looked at Maryanne. He was an un-healthy-looking man, skinny, like a bellows had been put to his mouth and opened and all the material of him sucked out, leaving only a gawky husk. He had large eyes that had survived the sucking, perfectly circular, and hair that might be faded with age or might simply be an undistinguished yellow-brown. 'Yes?' he said.

'I do not know anything, sir,' said Maryanne. 'Except that the baby is being seen by the doctor and its mother is there with it and Sarah Ward has taken a dreadful turn.' Her voice went high and the chaplain frowned.

'How old are you, girl?' he asked, but Maryanne did not wish to betray Sarah Ward again by not saying that she was twenty-one, and so she said nothing at all. 'Well?' said the chaplain. 'Speak!'

'Oh, leave her be,' said the woman holding the child. 'She's just a mousy little girl.'

'I pray you remember yourself, woman!' the chaplain said, offended, ineffectual. 'It is not for you to tell me to whom I might speak!' But he looked at Maryanne and, indeed, had nothing more to say to her at that time, and went away back through the door and up the ladder and through the hatch above.

IV

After the chaplain had gone Maryanne climbed carefully after him, away from the women who had directed their collective attention to her and expected her to understand something previously unspoken. She emerged into the bright clear air above bringing with her the restless feeling that she had left something behind, or left some important duty undone. It was Sarah Ward, of course, Sarah Ward there in her bed, white as the sheets, terrible blisters on her body, her hair gone garish red against her pallor.

The women were in their flocks again, seated together here and there. The girl with the womb trouble had curled herself up like a wounded cat on the deck near some matronly types who did not pay her any attention. Some women were picking at coarse stuff with needle and thread, and some others had their fingertips slipped into little books to mark their pages while they talked. Maryanne had no such pastime, and looked about, and found another of her little corners where she might go unnoticed. On her way there the ship dipped low and she darted sideways and gripped the rail for support. Despite this sudden buckling, the ocean was still entirely motionless to look at, like a great spill on the glassblower's floor that had been left to harden.

Others of the women cried fairly often but she had felt tears an impossibility, as if they had been shocked out of her at the instant of her creation as Maryanne Maginn. But now, looking again out at the desert of water, she found she had to tighten her mouth and throat and heart like fists inside her body against weeping. She stood there forcing the tears away.

The ship was their shelter, the small chalice carrying them through that which was inhospitable to human life. But there was no shelter for her there, she thought. There was only a series of confines between which she might move but never escape.

She understood this to be danger, when sadness and idleness might together unfix her from her present existence, from the all-that-there-is of the ship, and spin her backwards into those memories she could not entertain, not for the sake of her sanity, or spin her forward into anticipation of what was to come, which was to be a terror, most likely. Such dangers would occur. So now she did what she always did when her mind threatened her, which was to begin to think with great specificity of other things. What exactly this entailed depended on how she was occupied; at times she would count the back-and-forth of her scrubbing, or try to imagine the ship painted in different colours, or look at woman after woman and try to remember their names. Now, however, for lack of anything else, she began to tap her fingers. First twice, then four times, then eight, then sixteen, and she might have carried on into numbers so large they became mere abstractions when she was saved by the one who wished to save.

The chaplain had evidently thought of something to say to her, because he edged up to her right and placed one large-knuckled hand on the side, not far enough from hers for her liking. The way he had his hand on the rail meant his body was turned towards her and his left hand was unaccounted for, behind her. She dropped her eyes from the glass ocean to stare at her hands gripping the wood and his there beside them. 'Maryanne, child,' he said, softly, long-toothed and sincere. 'Every wise woman buildeth her house, but the foolish plucketh it down with her hands. Yes?'

'Yes, sir,' she murmured, and the stupidity of it was the thing that finally quashed the urge to weep and to remember. A calm came over her.

The chaplain repeated his words, more slowly. 'Every wise woman *buildeth* her house. But the foolish *plucketh* it down,' he said. 'What do you make of it?'

Maryanne paused. 'I think it very true,' she said, and he nodded beside her.

'Now, it is not really about the building of houses, is it?' the chaplain asked her.

'No, sir, I suppose it is not,' she said.

'What wisdom do you take from this?'

'I do not know, sir,' she said, humbly, and the chaplain smiled and looked out to sea.

'A wise woman…what does a wise woman do?'

'Buildeth her house,' she said, and the chaplain smiled again.

'Yes,' he said, patiently, 'but what is the meaning of it?'

Maryanne wrung her hands on the railing. His hand was too close; she wished to let go, but then she was afraid she would stumble against him if the movement of the ship surprised her. 'Well, sir, I suppose a wise woman creates, and a foolish woman destroys. But surely that is true of anybody,' she said.

The chaplain looked a little surprised. 'Yes,' he said, and then, for the second time that morning, he found himself with nothing more to say to her, and he patted the ship's railing twice and she felt his left hand hovering over her back, but he sidled away without going so far as to touch her.

Maryanne set her teeth. He was an idiot man; the proverb must certainly be about a wife, and her husband and children, and how she was to care for her family and her home and was therefore not relevant. He ought to have brought her the one about blessed is she that believed, or, no, better, the one about lowliness and meekness. Then a thought struck her.

'Sir?' she called after the chaplain, and he turned with a look of eagerness on his face. She kept her own face low as she said, 'I think that girl might need some help.'

'Which girl?'

'The one – you know, sir, the one who had a little trouble this morning.'

The chaplain reddened, and his eagerness fell away.

'Women's troubles are for the women. Now you remember what we have discussed,' he said, and left.

Maryanne closed her eyes a moment, then continued to her obscure corner to tuck herself away until dinner time.

Her corner gave her a good view of the hatch, and she watched as Lydia Sculthorpe's little boy was helped by the women coming up behind him, and last of all was the kind Irishwoman Joan Beattie. She watched as this woman went to the crate of their bedding and wrestled out a straw mattress and a blanket and dragged them towards the hatch. The little boy Sculthorpe had been standing lost and now came and picked up a trailing corner of the blanket and followed her with it. Joan smiled back at him. Then, glancing into the hatch, she had him help her push the bedding in, which was no help at all, so tiny was he, and then she climbed down after. He tried to go with her, but she said something to the other women, and they took him away. His eyes were like copper pennies.

The girl set herself to think of what she would think of, which would probably be Sarah Ward, although she did not know how to think of her without fear. Then that great rose of a woman Fernsby put her head up from below and climbed into the air, looking around. She had her dark hair tucked under her bonnet and was firmly done up in her mean clothing as they all must be, but she strolled like a lady at a garden party. 'Oh, Maginn, my dear,' she said. 'The doctor has found me to be a poor nurse and has asked for you instead.' Maryanne looked up at her. The sun was behind her, and her form was darkened. There was a flash, and Maryanne glanced over to see an officer had come to watch, brass-buttoned and cool. Fernsby gave no sign of seeing him. 'Come, dear,' she said, and waited while Maryanne got to her feet. 'He seems to think you shall do as you are told.'

Maryanne nodded. 'Yes, I shall.'

'Oh, no, Maginn! You must not,' said Fernsby, stooping a little to speak softly to her as they picked their way carefully back to the hatch. 'If the mother does not wish the doctor to blister the baby, or bleed her, or do any such cruelty, you must add your voice to hers and help her prevent him.'

'That is difficult,' said Maryanne.

'Not at all,' said Fernsby.

'But the doctor must know—'

'Blistering will not help the baby,' said Fernsby. 'Any fool knows you must not break the skin of a child. If he were a mother, he would know. I was bled once as a small child,' she added. 'It was not therapeutic. My mother always maintained it nearly killed me. And blistering is surely worse, for the pain is worse.'

In another life, perhaps Maryanne would have been good enough to brush Fernsby's hair or sit on a low stuffed stool by her chair by the fire and read to her, call her Miss or Madam, depending. She couldn't have been so great a lady, of course, given the circumstances. Or perhaps she had been, and none of the men in her family wanted to pay for her any more.

'It is the easiest thing in the world to do what is right, and hang the consequences,' Fernsby told her. 'Believe you me, you should prefer to be cast down in the coal-hole for a day or two knowing you have acted properly than to be sitting comfortably about, a traitor. The latter is bad for the spirit,' she said, and left her to go back down into the dark mouth of the hatch alone.

V

The berth she shared with Sarah Ward and two others was one of the less amenable, situated in the middle, far from either hatch. There the air lay sullen and thin, seeping in through the air scuttles high up in the bulkhead, too high to be of much use. The berths were built one above the other, and theirs was a lower. In the daytime the berths were nothing but wooden frames, with the bedding up on deck to air, partly for hygiene and partly so the women could not hide anything devious beneath their mattresses. Now, however, when Maryanne picked her way down the ladder and through the low labyrinthine room, she found that Joan Beattie had taken the bedding for their own berth, and that Sarah Ward returned from the hospital was lying there, clothed and bonneted.

Joan was kneeling beside her, and she looked up at Maryanne coming cautiously towards them.

'Did Miss Fernsby find you?' asked Joan.

'Yes, she did.'

Joan sighed and looked down at Sarah Ward. 'The doctor would not allow Sarah to stay,' she said softly. 'I do not think he cares for her. He has allowed that other woman to remain – the one who has been ill from the first day – and she has a temper, as I discovered when I tried to take her bedding to wash. But not Sarah.' She shook her head. 'It hurt her to move her. You little girls! Why are you here? You ought to be at home with your mothers,' she said, and then, 'If I were a mother my heart should just about tear out of my chest.' Maryanne came to kneel at Sarah Ward's other side, but Joan shook her head. 'He wants you to help with the baby. You had best go.'

Sarah lay stiffly, her skin grey. The only indication Maryanne could see that she was not dead was the tension in her, the tightness with which her eyes were closed and the quivering lines of her body. Maryanne came a little closer, wanting to look at Sarah's throat, maybe, or more closely at her face, but Joan Beattie said, 'Go!' and so she skittered off to the hospital to do as she was told, except for when she mustn't.

. . .

The air in the hospital was closer than before, and Sarah Ward's bed was yet unmade, although the one where Fernsby had been lying was tucked tight and smooth. The curly head of the woman who was always sick and might die was still there, her face and body hidden beneath the blanket. The mother, Lydia Sculthorpe, was standing leaning against a bulkhead, her hands now at her throat, watching, horrified, as the doctor peered over her baby. He looked up at Maryanne and came over to take her elbow and guide her away. She felt a shock at being touched by him, his hand large and foreign, but he did it casually, like he was moving some small item to a position more convenient. 'Maginn,' he said. 'The baby is ill. I must administer a blister to each leg. You can read, can you not, and you have a steady hand? You can comprehend and carry out a direction if I give it to you?'

'Yes, sir,' she said.

'Sculthorpe,' said the doctor, to the mother. 'Maginn will assist in the application of the blister powder.'

'No,' the mother said, rushing to the bed and standing over her baby as if to ward him off. 'No, Doctor, you will not wear me down, sir. You cannot do that to her.'

'Foolish!' the doctor cried, slapping the bulkhead by Maryanne's shoulder, making her wince. He pointed a thick grey fungus of a finger at Lydia Sculthorpe. 'My patience is continually tested! You mark my words: if that infant dies, it will be not from illness but from your inanity and the conspiracy of women.' He strode off to a tall desk and opened a brown journal there, leafing through it, and, finding his page, ran his finger down a column, then began to take some brisk notes with a fine gold pen.

Maryanne moved quietly over to Lydia Sculthorpe and her baby. 'What is the baby's name?' she whispered.

'Mary,' Lydia Sculthorpe whispered back. 'Have you seen my little lad? Are they taking care of him?'

'Yes, they are... he is above decks with them now.'

'What are you whispering about?' asked the doctor, his voice clipped.

'We are praying, sir,' spat Lydia Sculthorpe, and the doctor glanced back at them. 'He does not know that we are human beings,' she said to Maryanne, dropping her voice once more as he turned away. 'He does not know *she* is a human being.' And she kissed the baby's head, then bunched the blanket in her hands so violently her knuckles went white.

'Maginn, will you discover the name of the infant, for my notes,' said the doctor flatly, still writing.

'She is called Mary Sculthorpe, sir,' answered Maryanne.

'How do you know?' he asked, pausing in his writing and turning to look at her again.

'I asked, sir.'

The doctor looked at Maryanne a little longer before turning back to his notes. 'Mary Sculthorpe,' he said, writing, and then, 'Age?'

'Three months,' said Lydia Sculthorpe, and the doctor stood still, his back yet to them, and they both understood at once that they were waiting for Maryanne to repeat this information, for he had decided like a churlish schoolboy not to listen to Lydia.

'Three months,' said Maryanne, and he wrote this down with a flourish.

'Fernsby took it upon herself to put the cantharides powder away,' he said. 'Fetch it from the drawer.' He briskly indicated a cabinet on the flat wall by the door. 'Can – tha – rides,' he repeated. 'C – A – N – and so forth.'

Maryanne glanced at Lydia Sculthorpe and her baby again, then went over. The cabinet was a sturdy item of dark wood, bolted to the floor and walls. She opened the doors and sighed a little at the many fussy drawers within, each marked with a card written in fresh ink. The drawer marked CANTHARIDES was right in the middle, right before her eyes. She began opening drawers, other drawers, to packets and tins and bundles of linen, and closing them again.

'What are you doing?' the doctor asked Maryanne, and she looked back at him watching her, carefully closing both lids on his travel inkwell, and so she opened the correct drawer and took out a little tin. She glanced over at the windows, which did not open, of course, and at Lydia Sculthorpe leaning on the bed with her arms lightly about her baby, and she took the cap off the tin and poured the entirety of the brown powder into her own left palm. Then, holding this powder carefully, she put the tin and its cap back in the drawer with her right hand and closed the drawer, and the cabinet doors, then brought her right hand down and began rubbing the blister powder between her palms and thoroughly over her fingers too. She let the great excess of it drift to her skirt and the floor, and although the doctor overcame his shock and lurched towards her, the burning had already begun.

VI

She knew herself to be underwater. Although she could breathe, it was a cautious breathing, as though her air might be stopped at any time. The creak of the ship was different down here; it was more of an act of resistance than the simple shifting and settling of above decks. The officer led Maryanne, while Peter Rowe the Cornish sailor quietly followed with a lantern. The officer bent fluidly, unbolted the hatch at his feet and swung it open. A hot light arose from below.

'Go down,' said the officer, so she went, backwards, quiet. Her hands in their wrapped linen bandage smarted against the wooden rungs, and the thick glass bottle of water that hung on a cord about her neck swung awkwardly. She descended into a place of oily light, rich with golden and dark wood, planks stacked high and curls of it like autumn leaves beneath her feet. The walls and low ceiling were tacked with tools in firm brackets, and a large bench under an overhang was so crowded with these tools and pieces of wood that she did not at first see the carpenter himself gnomed up under there, over his work, three lanterns ablaze, until he pushed something away from him and turned to watch them come. His eyes sparked under a low and shining brow. He asked her something, but he spoke so low and fast she could not understand him. Peter Rowe shook his head and the carpenter, smiling a little, ducked back down to his labours. The officer cleared his throat, but the exchange had passed him by, apparently, because when he spoke it was to ask her about Fernsby. 'What is her name?' he asked. 'Her Christian name?'

'I do not know, sir,' said Maryanne.

'Hmm.' He brought her over to another hatch, sweeping it of wood shavings with his boot and stooping to unbolt and swing it open. 'Go down,' he said, again, but this time the hole was dark, and Peter Rowe held the lantern out over the hatch that she might see the ladder. She stood a short while but then crouched and took herself backwards and down into a small and tarry hold filled with bundled rope of

all sizes. The officer and then Peter Rowe came down
after her, although there was so little room to stand
Peter Rowe remained hanging on the ladder to hold
the lantern above them. She checked her bottle; the
cork was firmly in place, the water right up to it. She
had the thought of escaping up and up into the open
air to perhaps throw herself into the ocean, but the
hard glass of the water she had seen would surely not
yield to her anyway.

'The carpenter ought to have natural light,' mused
the officer, apparently to Peter Rowe, who said, 'Aye,
sir.'

'I shall mention it to the captain,' the officer added.

The smell in the little hold was dense with the
mustiness of tar. The groans of the ship were like
those of an injured animal, but far away, and muffled.
'Step aside,' said the officer, and she saw that there was
another hatch below her feet. 'This is the final one,' he
said as she shuffled back against the bundles of rope,
and he bent to unfasten the bolt and swing the hatch
open. She looked up, to delay witnessing the place she
was to go. Looking up meant looking at Peter Rowe,
but the lantern was between them and so all she had
was his silhouette. So she looked down. There was another ladder and another well of black, but the lantern

did not dispel it. 'Go down,' the officer told her, and she took a breath and went and knelt by the ladder and dropped her legs in backwards to begin her final descent. The cold of it welled up at her. The room with the ropes was warm, but down below was a deep and inhuman iciness.

She looked back up at Peter Rowe, who did not leer at her and who had once asked her name. Now her position had shifted she could see his face, although she could not read his expression. 'Bear up,' he said, holding the light out and down. 'Go elsewhere in your mind. Whatever place you have in there that is pleasant.'

Maryanne thought the officer might not like his talking to her, but the officer in his brass buttons was scarcely paying attention, his hands in his pockets, gazing ruminatively at the rope as he waited. 'A fine woman,' he mused. 'Remarkable that she is amongst your kind.'

'I cannot do it,' said Maryanne, hearing the scurrying of rats below. The shift of the boat tried to pull her from the ladder so forcefully that she clung to it, not moving.

'Come, girl,' said the officer, shaking his head not in disapproval but to clear it of his daydreaming, it seemed. 'I must get back. They told me you destroyed medicine with which the doctor was to treat an infant child. Go down and take your punishment, for you may find you are the better for it when you come back up again.'

'May I keep the light?' she asked, still clinging to the ladder.

'What! No! You would set the entire ship on fire,' said the officer. 'Go down now, and no more silliness. Many have gone down before you and arisen again well chastened.'

And so she went, hand below hand, looking up at Peter Rowe bearing the light above until she set her feet on the coal which rattled and shifted and she sank nearly to her knees. The officer flipped the hatch shut and all light was extinguished with such suddenness and extremity her eyes stung. The drawing of the bolt was a low, slow grating. Then she heard the voice of the officer ordering Peter Rowe back up, and there were no more sounds from above. She breathed a deep and trembling breath, tasting coal dust, feeling it in her throat. 'Shall I be forgotten or remembered?' she asked the air.

She stood holding the ladder for some time in that perfect blackness, perfect freezing solitude, until she shifted the coal and let her knees find the floor. She knelt leaning against the rungs of the ladder, her legs pressed in by hard-edged coal, uncomfortable but anchored. She shut her eyes as if she might fool herself that the darkness was her own doing. She kept still, except that she kicked her feet from time to time to keep the rats away. And to remind herself that she could indeed move, and was not half-buried alive.

First she became distracted by the idea that she was still wearing Joan Beattie's shawl. She ought to have given it back, she chided herself, before being taken below. Truly, though, she was glad to have it for the warmth, and for the smell of sheep, which gave her hope that somewhere out there in the world there were still green fields. But that comfort did also bring a bitterness, because it necessarily reminded her that someone had been kind to her, and had performed for her an act of care of which she was probably not worthy, which was almost too much for her to think about. And so she made herself stop worrying about the shawl, which also took away the green fields. And that left her there in the blackness. So then she began to revisit the instant in the hospital when she had poured out the blister dust. She ought to have pretended to stumble, and dropped it, and then maybe she would not be here now.

She thought of Joan Beattie talking about how young she and Sarah Ward were, how they ought to be with their mothers, but before that thought could lead her mind to the mother of the dead girl with the French name, she felt something tug at her skirt. It was minute but undeniable, and she shrieked and grappled with the ladder, her hands sore, not knowing which way was climbing and which way was falling, scrabbling, coal dust thickening, until finally she managed to bring herself up off the deck to hang on the rungs as Peter Rowe had with the lantern. She was afraid that somehow in her confusion she had uncorked the bottle, maybe, or damaged it, but when she took it in her hands it was cold and smooth and replete, the cork still in place.

Rats can climb better than you can, she thought, then, Do not think of it.

Her heart was beating so fast and loud that she was afraid she would not hear the scurryings of the rats again and would not notice if they came close. She did not know how to quiet her heart there as she clung to the ladder against the roll of the ship, so to distract herself, she began to sing the one song she could recall.

It was 'Early One Morning', which was a pretty tune but had been sung too often by the women after their dinner when they were feeling ruminative, or above decks in the sunset when the chaplain was busy off saving some girl or other, until they had been told to sing something else because the captain was growing irritated. Maryanne could not recall all the words, and so sang the first few lines over and over, either for minutes or hours, until her mouth was dry. And then there she was again, in the blackness.

She wanted water badly, but didn't dare, in case she became confused once more and spilt the lot of it. Her heart had quietened now, and so she listened again for rats, and she heard them too, scratching and rustling. Then she came to understand she could hear something else as well, and her heart quickened once more, and she felt a kind of plunging in her soul. The creaking of the ship had been masking it, perhaps, but now all at once it was perfectly clear. She first told herself it was rats, then ropes, but then she could think of nothing else it might be but a baby crying, and she knew it had been crying for some time, perhaps even the entire time. It was Lydia Sculthorpe's baby, of course, and the crying was not a bad sign, for crying was a sign of life, and of lungs that would fill with air. The trouble with this idea was that the crying was coming from down somewhere below her feet. Her breasts began to prickle with milk and that aching came into her arms again, and she knew and had always known it to be the ache of emptiness, the ache of a particular absence, and she gasped in a great breath and let go of the ladder and dropped down into the coal, twisting her foot, banging her shoulder, scraping her face, and scrabbling around to find her own little lost baby whose cries were growing worse and worse.

Her heart was going fast again, but even the banging of it and the tumbling of the coal and her own shrieks could do nothing to drown out the crying. But wherever she moved her hands there was only coal, or wood. Once she touched a warm body, but it was furry and it darted away. She dived after it and banged into a bulkhead, or perhaps the deck, or the ladder, or something, and the bottle around her neck clacked and cracked and cold water soaked right through the shawl and her bodice and shift and slapped against her skin. Now there was broken glass, too, and a broken bottleneck about her own neck, but she continued flailing around, calling out, scratching and crawling, and the crying went on, always below, always beyond, until she banged again into something, hard, with her head, and for the first time down there she saw a flash of light, but it was only for an instant.

The crying was gone, like a mouse into a snake's mouth.

For a confusing time, she thought she was home. Truly home, in the place she had decided she would not remember, where the light was soft through curtains. Her mother sat by her bed and talked to her until she fell asleep. Never stories, but terrible, dry things, like how to decline various verbs in Latin or French, or how to go about growing a flower garden, or how to make bobbin lace. So she lay in her bed and her mother sat by and filled that dizzy silence with talk.

'In order to make a lace collar, you will need certain items,' her mother said. 'One, many silk threads. Two, a set of bobbins. Three, a straw-filled cushion. Four, a piece of card. Five, many pins. Now, there are three kinds of lace you may make with bobbins. The first is straight lace, in which the lacemaker might employ a great number of bobbins in order to produce lace in one piece. Next, we come to part lace. Part lace is an amusing method of making lace with the help of a friend, for it is worked in pieces and later joined in a manner I shall latterly describe. Finally, we have braid lace. Braid lace uses fewer bobbins than its two counterparts and is thus more economical.'

The girl lay listening to her mother with the glowing curtains drawn against the hush of early twilight in the village, and she blinked softly and was then in bed in the hospital, and she felt many hours or perhaps days had passed, but she could not account for them. She looked over and saw the curly head of the woman who was always ill bundled with the covers all over the rest of her. This woman slowly uncurled and rolled onto her back, and the girl could see the great mound of a pregnant belly below the blankets.

It hurt to move her head. Her hands hurt, too, and her ankle, and elsewhere. Then she closed her eyes and fell asleep again. When next she woke she thought to turn her sore head the other way and look for Lydia Sculthorpe and her baby, but they were not there. She was terribly thirsty, and she remembered the black hole and the crying in it, and tried to push herself out of bed so she could go back down there and look again, maybe with a lantern, this time. Maybe with Peter Rowe to help her. But the act of sitting upright made her spurt a yellow fluid from her mouth directly across the bedclothes. Someone with soft hands brought water to her lips, and she drank and then fell asleep again. The next time she woke up she thought of the black hole once again, but this time her head felt clearer and she understood there was nothing down there other than rats and coal, and so she lay still, waiting for what would next be done.

VII

'There is an entire sky out there,' said Sarah Ward, musingly, looking through the little squares of window behind the beds. Maryanne gazed and gazed at her, too sore to move or reach a bandaged hand to Sarah. She could not see the windows, but it felt like it was night-time. The lantern above swayed golden, the light sliding back and forth over Sarah, pulling at the shadows of her face. Her white cap framed her face sweetly, softening the sharpness, red hair wisping out. She looked thin, and a little tired.

'What?' Sarah snapped. 'What are you looking at?'

'Are you alive?'

'Oh Lord, yes,' said Sarah. 'I will never die. I am a spirit.'

'Is that true?'

'Yes! What – do you think a spirit would lie?'

'I suppose not.'

'No! I am an undying spirit, and sometimes I need to try and get as close to death as I can so that I might understand what you mere mortals must face. Otherwise I could not live amongst you. I would be too lofty.'

A terrible pressure came away from Maryanne's body and she felt so light she might rise from the bed.

'That girl Mary Piper with the womb trouble is sick, but she does not want us to tell the doctor,' said Sarah Ward.

'Why not?'

'Why do you think? You know where her trouble is! She does not want his hands up there again.'

'That is fair,' said Maryanne dreamily. 'I am in your place, and you in mine,' she added, the warm light dipping and sliding.

'Do you mean you were sitting here while I was lying where you are? Yes. This stool's a fright,' said Sarah, wiggling. 'How did you sit so straight? Damn it. I hate a seat without a back.' She stood abruptly and pushed Maryanne's legs aside so she could half-recline on the narrow bed, leaning heavily on her. It hurt, and was good. 'This is scarcely better,' she said. 'For a little thing, you take up a good deal of room. Why do we not get chairs?'

'Because we do not deserve them,' said Maryanne.

'Yes. We are too foul for chairs.'

'Yes.'

'Chairs are for the pure-hearted.'

'Yes.' They smiled at one another, and Maryanne felt her lips crack.

'You look as if you have lost a fight with a tiger,' said Sarah.

'Perhaps I have.'

'Oh, do not get poetic with me. I know you were wrestling yourself down in the coal-hole.'

'Am I filthy?' asked Maryanne.

'I should think so,' said Sarah slyly, which Maryanne did not quite understand, although it made her blush.

'I mean do I have coal dust on me?'

'No. That Beattie woman washed you.'

Maryanne nodded and said, thick-voiced, 'I was afraid you would die.'

'And that is why you were rolling around in the coal?'

'No – but I was afraid for you regardless.'

Sarah waved a dismissive hand. It seemed too loose, like the flesh and veins and all the matter keeping her wrists together had been eaten away by the poison she had taken, leaving her hand to simply flap on a bare joint. 'We have already addressed that matter. I am an undying spirit. Why were you at yourself down there?' But Maryanne could not find the words to say, and she watched as Sarah Ward grew bored above her. 'Never mind,' said Sarah, standing and stretching her fingertips high before brushing down the front of her dress. 'I ain't supposed to be in here, so I ought to creep back now and curl up next to our dear berthmates and dream of your friend the sailor from Cornwall. I need a sponge up my petticoats when I think of him or I get all greasy.'

Maryanne needed to say something to keep her there. 'That woman is pregnant,' she said, desperately.

'Which one?'

'The one there, who will likely die.'

At this, the woman in the next bed with the chestnut hair groaned and rolled her bulk over. 'No,' she said. 'I will not die.' Her eyes were as glazed and wide and unseeing as a pair of cracked eggs.

'Oh! Forgive me!' said Maryanne. 'I did not know you were awake.'

Sarah Ward was laughing at her, but even as she laughed, she was casting around. 'Where is the water? None in here? That is poorly done of the doctor. I will go out to the dipper and get you some, but I will have to feel my way, so if I spill it you will have to go thirsty,' she said, either to Maryanne or the other woman, or both, and was gone, and she must have spilt the water, Maryanne thought, because she did not return that night.

There was then a dream of sitting by a red fire set in a brick hearth. The flames swayed and snapped. She was on a worn jute rug, very plain and poor, but the room she was in was otherwise in complete darkness. The fire entranced her, flames flickering and darting like hot little tongues. But then from the room behind her a shuffling came, a shuffling towards her. It was a sound like somebody ailing in stiff silk and slippers. She could not turn around, and she felt the air on her neck begin to move, to whisper against her skin. She watched as slowly from the quiet darkness beside her came a pair of white hands holding open a great bellows. The hands moved forward and she saw the arms, the black sleeves, and then they stopped, so the face and body were hidden in the dark. There was a breathing, and the hands tightened and squeezed the bellows down, and a shining purple thing came ballooning from the end, larger and larger until it suckered away from the bellows and fell to sizzle wetly in the fire. The breathing grew louder and the hands continued to press the bellows down and out came a red thing like a birth, a bloody circle that fell. Next, a long snake of more glistening purple and white went coiling into the fire. These things, these organs, were so wet and heavy that the fire started to go out.

When next she woke the doctor told her it was Sunday and she must get up and make her bed and dress properly and go up on deck for prayers. Lydia Sculthorpe was in the hospital again, lying with her baby in her arms. Maryanne floated, unfixed.

On deck, the wind had picked up and the sails snapped above them like clean sheets. The women knelt, behind them the officers on chairs. Sarah Ward darted her a quick look which was to say, 'See? *They* get chairs.' Sailors stood behind those seated.

The children were restless. Their mothers were trapped in constant movement, winding the little bodies over and over themselves.

Unbandaged, Maryanne's hands had barely blistered, for the cantharides powder had not had long enough to take such effect, but still they were pink and raw. Her neck was scratched and had come up in scabs, and her ankle was tender to walk upon. Her head ached, and ached more when she bent it to pray.

The chaplain was intoning something irrelevant not only to them but to most of humanity. 'For the priesthood being changed,' he said, 'there is made of necessity a change also of the law. For he of whom these things are spoken pertaineth to another tribe, of which no man gave attendance at the altar.'

Maryanne was praying that poem again, that Water, water. Water, water, everywhere. At least that could not be argued with when you were on a boat, and being correct brings a kind of satisfaction.

Sarah Ward leant against her. 'I am to help with the cooking this week,' she whispered. 'It is not yet my turn, but the doctor thinks I need honest occupation.' Then, when Maryanne nodded tightly but did not reply, she continued, 'He has decided we shan't be put down the coal-hole any more, after your great performance. He's going to have the carpenter build a special little box to lock us in, to be kept up on deck where we might be watched.' A small boy beside her made a leap from his mother's arms and knocked her, and so she knocked into Maryanne, and they swayed together.

'Maginn!' said the chaplain, loud and sharp. 'Silence!' The women kept their heads down.

'It was me, sir,' said Sarah Ward, lifting her face to him. He did not know what to do with that act of honest fellowship, and so he hemmed and hawed and finally ignored it and read on. Sarah dropped her head again, but Maryanne saw her hidden smile.

A toddler sitting on her mother's lap lurched to the side and escaped, the mother and the women around grabbing for her. The child scrambled to Maryanne and launched herself at her. The mother stooped in, scooping the child, dipping herself to the chaplain. 'I had better take her, sir…' she was saying, and the chaplain waved her off, and off she went, triumphant, it seemed, sending amused looks to her friends. She backed down the hatch, holding the girl over her shoulder. Meanwhile, the little Sculthorpe boy with eyes like copper pennies began to wail for his mother, and several other children cried because he was crying.

'Yes! Very well!' the chaplain cried, his voice rising and cracking to be heard. 'All children must be taken below!'

There was murmuring from the officers behind them. The women darted after their own children and wrestled them away, making their way backwards down the hatch with little ones writhing over them. And so Maryanne and Sarah Ward and perhaps only half of the women remained to listen about many priests and the changing of laws thereunto.

'Sir, do we have souls?' asked Sarah Ward, right over the intonations of the chaplain. He looked up with a flash of malice, though he again did not reply and instead continued his reading. But the assuredness had gone from his voice. He stood before them, saying his words, his book wilting from his hands, impotent and wretched. Even his words limped into silence, though, when the gentle young countrywoman from Suffolk arose from below and asked if any of the women remaining above decks were midwives, because the one who might die was in labour.

The old witch Mary Christie grunted and shuffled and creaked her body up. 'I am she,' she said, and limped away and down with her limbs folded like an old bird.

VIII

At first it was the impulse of many to laugh at the cries winding out from behind the closed hospital door and throughout their quarters. It was laughter of the hard kind they had, although it was not cruel exactly. Knowing, perhaps. But then the hours wore on, and they were not allowed back above decks and were not told why not, and the cries grew worse. And so the laughter died, and silence fell amongst the women, although the children grew irritable and wept often.

Lydia Sculthorpe crept out from the hospital and amongst them, her bodice all undone and her baby suckling. Her friends opened their arms to her and she went down couched amongst them. Her toddler son, who had been sleeping against another woman, moaned and wailed and tottered to collapse onto her other breast and went quiet again.

Mary Piper wandered to her berth and stood look-ing at it. Without its mattress and bedding, it offered nothing but hard planks. She stood before it, then leant forward until her forehead was pressed against the berth above it. Finally, she folded her body down onto the planks and lay on her side with her knees up against her chest. 'She is an odd girl,' whispered someone.

With little talk, and no songs, the hours stretched like slow treacle. The birthing woman began to groan, deep and close, like some beast of the field in useless distress. Dinner time crept upon them. Those who were that week preparing and serving the food leapt to their feet and were gone too long and returned with dragging feet and reluctant hands under their great trays of afternoon rations. The salt mutton was tougher even than usual and they were chewing and chewing as the woman lowed and groaned. They were given an extra ration of wine, even Maryanne, and Sarah Ward, whose wine rations had been stopped. Maryanne drank hers quick. Joan Beattie took some to Mary Piper curled up on the boards, but Mary would not drink. The plush, coarse young woman called Elizabeth Duncan whom the captain took for himself every night and sometimes in the day came down and whispered that even he could hear the screams from the hospital, all the way up above them. She looked frightened.

A particular feeling had come upon Maryanne. It was a feeling of rising up out of herself and looking back down at her own body little and brittle and crabbed in agony. A feeling of something breaking most terribly, like a translucent porcelain dish put under such pressure it burst into dust. And an utter sense of abjection, of the inside come out.

They sat there drinking their wine, the silences welling deep and taut only to be broken by the beastlike calling from beyond the hospital door. The women who were cleaners took their dishes and cups back into the large trays to take away and wash, and still nobody was saying much. A few were praying. The babies cried. Sarah Ward went primly to the water closet to be ill.

Finally the chaplain came and told them they might go above. In a flow like a white-capped river, everybody climbed into the golden air. Lydia Sculthorpe and her children went supported on either side by friends, and Mary Piper came shuffling behind.

Above decks, the sun spread like oil over the broad water. The ship was a trembling handful of sticks.

The women were pinning themselves together now, pressed close in their muted circles. Lydia Sculthorpe sat like the Madonna holding her sickly baby, head nodding, her son draped over her knee.

Maryanne sat close with Sarah Ward, Joan Beattie, Elizabeth Duncan whom the captain took and Mary Piper, who was wet and dank with sweat, and two or three others. They were directly on the deck, knee to knee, shoulder to shoulder, warm and soft. Looking up at them, and around at the others, Maryanne saw a kind of vapour rising into the low, golden air. Barely visible forces were exiting the dark of their bodies to hang about them and map themselves for all to see, so any one of them might glance at another or hear her name and gain immediate access to all kinds of information about her, about what she would think of some matter, what she would choose, and how she would feel. Maryanne saw this and knew it had always been there. A soft wing beat in her heart.

The sun fell softly and pooled their faces in shadow under their bonnets, but Joan Beattie lifted her face to it. She was wearing her brown shawl. It was clean.

'Did I not dirty that?' asked Maryanne. 'I did not mean to wear it down into the coal-hole.'

'I have washed it, my dear,' said Joan Beattie. 'I hope it gave you a little warmth.'

A scream came distant from below.

'May I wear it?' whispered Mary Piper, then cleared her throat and said too loudly, 'I am freezing cold.' Her skin was red and glistening but she hugged her arms about herself, and Joan Beattie unwrapped herself and draped the shawl over the girl's shoulders. 'You really ought to go to the doctor,' she said, but Mary shook her head tightly.

Elizabeth Duncan, fat on meat from the captain's table, asked Joan Beattie why she had never married.

'You shouldn't ask that,' said a wan girl with a baby in each arm. She was red-haired, like Sarah Ward, but her hair was limper and duller than Sarah's.

A woman languidly unfolded from a row on a bench against the far railing and strolled towards them; it was Fernsby, with her socialite's sense for gossip.

'She can ask,' said Joan Beattie, and sighed, and moved herself sideways to allow Fernsby to rest herself down amongst them to listen. 'We might as well talk. It is no great tragedy. Betsy Duncan here has asked me why I did not ever marry,' she said to Fernsby.

'Good heavens,' said Fernsby, civilly, and the birthing woman moaned up through the boards.

'I *was* to marry, in fact. When I was seventeen or eighteen I was engaged to a soldier who gave me a little ring with a stone in it,' Joan Beattie said, drawing a small circle in the air as if to indicate the shape of the stone. 'A little green stone. I liked him. But then my brother's wife – they lived in Liverpool – she died, and you know they had children, eight of them I think, no, nine, and she died having the tenth, so I had to go off from Ireland to Liverpool and live with my brother and care for the children and there was no room for the soldier, because then I would have had children of my own and it would have been too many, and I would not have been able to care for my nieces and nephews too, even if he had wanted to come to Liverpool with me. He was English, so perhaps he might have. But I didn't ask him to. And I suppose he didn't say it, either.'

Their little circle fell quiet, but then Sarah Ward surprised Maryanne and perhaps all of them by saying, with some tenderness, 'You'd have made a fine mother, Joan Beattie.'

Joan smiled, but then another cry came from below, and her smile slipped away, and she looked out at the water.

'It is a funny thing to feel, you know. I raised those

children and loved them like my own, and yet here I am, alone.'

'That is for the best,' said Sarah Ward.

'What will they do with her if she dies? Or the baby?' whispered Elizabeth Duncan, and they shushed her. 'Oh, I'm forever saying the wrong thing!' she said, and crossed her arms tightly. 'I ain't wishing them dead!'

'They'll put them over the side,' said Joan Beattie.

'Into the water?'

'Yes.'

There was another lull, and Maryanne felt them all listening and trying not to listen for cries from below, but there were none. 'How deep is the sea?' she asked.

'Oh, fathoms and fathoms,' said Joan.

'What's a fathom?' asked Elizabeth Duncan, but Sarah Ward talked a little over her to say instead, 'I hate it here. It's a *bad* fucking God *damned* place.'

'Yes, my dear,' said Joan, and placed a gentle hand on her knee then took it away again. 'You know…' she began, but she grew distracted by the sight of the mushroomy doctor emerging up from a hatch beyond their pen and making his way to the grand door that had the captain's rooms somewhere behind it. The women all watched him go into the darkness of the doorway, his broad back blinking out like a tired eye.

'What?' said Sarah Ward.

'What?' said Joan Beattie.

'You were going to tell us something more.'

Joan shifted her weight, easing her legs from under her. 'Yes,' she said. 'Goodness me, this kneeling does my knees no favours!' she added. 'I suppose the doctor has left the women's business to the women.'

The girl with the twins nodded. 'He should not be there,' she said. 'The best thing in the world for a birth is a wise woman. No one wants a man's big dirty hands down there.' Sarah Ward smirked and Maryanne knew she was about to say that *she* wanted a man's big dirty hands down there, but another scream came from below and she did not say it.

'Will you tell us what you were going to tell us, Joan Beattie?' asked Maryanne, and Joan smiled.

'Well – it is that when my little brothers and sisters would die, you know, my mother used to say their spirits were flying to Heaven and their bodies being received into the earth,' she said, musingly, to none of them in particular. There are people like this, Maryanne thought, who know when a story is needed. 'Or perhaps she would say their bodies were *joining* the earth – I cannot remember the exact word she used,' Joan went on. 'But I do remember the impression I formed of this in my young head, and it was a peaceful imagining, that my brother or my sister would be lying on soft, sweet grass, green as green, green as an emerald, and a little white winged thing would come out of their mouths, not a bird but winged, with bird's wings, feathered but no beak, no eyes, and swoop off and away into the sky, quick as a flash. And then I imagined that my brother or my sister would begin to sink gently into the grass, and – they were peaceful, you know, asleep, in my mind – that the earth would become soft, just like – you know, as if it were milk pudding, or something like that – and it would pool and my brother or my sister would go gently in and it would close back over them and there would be a lump which would then sink down and the grass would be just as soft and green and sweet as it had been before. Where I lived there were fields of grass like this. Before I was sent to Liverpool, which is a dirty great place, there were fields, and I imagined all the little children and everybody who had died down there. And although I had seen the coffins go many times into the dirt of the churchyard, I could not picture any person I loved, or any person at all, in that sad place. Instead I would close my eyes and pretend we had carried that person out onto the grass and laid them down there, not in any box at all, to be – yes – received.'

Sarah Ward had been watching her as she spoke. 'Why are you here, Joan Beattie?' she asked her. 'You're too good for the likes of us.' Sarah's face was shining, her cheeks rosy, her eyes clear. Maryanne had never seen her so well. She had a sudden, vivid picture in her mind's eye of Sarah Ward as she ought to be, wearing a low green dress and laughing in a public house, perhaps, by a hot hearth.

Joan began to peacefully say, 'Well, my dear…' but she stopped when Mary Christie put her wry white head up from below decks and showed them all her bloody hands.

'A girl,' Mary said, grinning, and gave a shout of triumph that made them laugh. 'Hearty and hale, and the mother sitting up and eating bread and butter. It is the way, sometimes,' Mary Christie the witch went on, never saner, putting a neighbourly elbow on the hatch as she stood there, half below and half above. 'They are sometimes sick right until the end, then at last the babe comes and all is well.' A great exhalation came from all the women together.

Into this air of relief there was a sharp rap; it was the carpenter's hammer against the gate of their pen. The women tensed into one another again. Maryanne remembered the carpenter looking at her as she was taken below, and she felt the cold of the coal-hole once again all over her body. But Sarah Ward was holding her hand.

The carpenter had come amongst them with two men carrying a large box like a coffin, each one bearing a narrow end, so they were separated by the length of it. He led these men directly through the midst of the women, looking openly at their faces and bodies with his nail-head eyes as he did so. The men went slowly, watching one another rather than the women, so the women in their path were compelled to not only part for them but also to duck their bonneted heads for fear of hard corners.

'Don't worry yourselves,' the carpenter told them, raising his eyebrows, his mouth twisted. 'I have built you your nice little locking box that will hold you when you sin, until you're sorry for it and your souls are much recovered.'

Maryanne looked around for the chaplain, whose only real use was preventing men from speaking to them, but he had withdrawn himself, just like the doctor.

Mary Christie waggled her red fingers at the carpenter.

'What name will she give the baby?' called Fernsby, ignoring the men.

'Astraea,' said Mary Christie, and the women nodded as if this were only to be expected, although Maryanne was sure she had never heard such a name before.

'Let us hear her surname as well, so we may know how it sounds,' said someone.

'Astraea Pitchfork.'

'What!' said Sarah Ward. 'What manner of name is Pitchfork?'

'It is her family name,' said Mary Christie, arch, now patting herself here and there and finally drawing a yellow-stained handkerchief from the pocket of her apron. She began to wipe her bloody hands. 'She says she comes from a long line of Pitchforks.' Then, looking directly at Maryanne, she said, 'Her milk has not come in.'

IX

The baby Astraea Pitchfork was a pleated, wiry little creature, her skin flaking and folded, pasted with blood and white wax, her mouth red, her face formed on rage. Her arms moved in jerks, like a puppet on strings poorly handled by its master, and the limp purple tail of the cord lay on her belly. And yet she fit as naturally into the crook of Maryanne's arm as if she were a part of her very body.

Maryanne sat dumbly on an empty bed holding the baby, while Mary Christie undid her bodice and took her hard little breast in crooked fingers and gave it a good and practised squeeze. Hot milk sprayed and the baby nuzzled her face back and forth until she felt the nipple and began to suck. Maryanne felt her whole self pour into that greedy mouth. Relief, relief. The pulling of the thorn, the bursting of the blister. The mother in the next bed watched hungrily.

Mary Christie limped off to get one of the stools Sarah Ward so hated and sat herself between them. There was no trace of her madness about her now, whether it had been feigned or real. She was steady with purpose.

Outside the squares of windows the sea sucked away the sun, and the milk-white stars leaked into the dark of the sky.

'Have you wet-nursed before?' asked the new mother Pitchfork, her voice hoarse from screaming.

'No,' said Maryanne.

'That having of a baby is a dreadful wonder,' she said. 'I can't believe you've done it too. You're such a little lass.'

'Yes, it is dreadful,' said Maryanne.

'But where is your baby?' asked Pitchfork. She was not as young as Maryanne, but not much older either. Despite having grown too thin, she was pretty, her face bright and raw after her agony, her eyes large and dark. Someone had plaited her brown hair around her head.

The baby smelt of that thing she could not describe. It was like slipping sighing into warm water. She felt her muscles do the remembering for her. 'My baby is with my mother,' she said.

'Boy or girl?'

'Boy.'

'Name?'

Maryanne paused. 'I did not give him one,' she said. 'They did not allow it.' She paused again. 'I hope my mother named him something sensible.'

The stars outside the window were cold and perfect, presented like little square pictures of stars in their panes of glass. She could see no moon. The baby sucked and sucked, one breast and then the other.

'You must keep trying, with the milk,' Mary Christie said to the mother.

The baby slowed and stopped her sucking and vomited some curds onto Maryanne and all at once was asleep, her lips still on the nipple.

'If you stop, your milk will never come. I will see if I can get you some cream to drink.' Then, to Maryanne, she said, 'Sleep here in the hospital. We will need you again in the night.'

But then the hatch above was opened clumsily and the doctor climbed down, the sky against his head, his clothing dishevelled and his face red, like a man come home from a hot tavern or a brothel. 'No, you may not sleep here,' he said, his voice so loud and deep all three women looked, alarmed, at the sleeping baby in Maryanne's arms, but she did not stir. 'Christie, you will fetch Maginn from her berth if she is needed in the night.'

As Maryanne slipped out, her breasts light and dry, Lydia Sculthorpe shuffled half-asleep into the warm light, her baby still bundled in her arms. 'It is happening again, sir,' she said.

Maryanne stood there with the darkness at her back, the night women and their children all laid out in their berths like bodies after a disaster.

'Go to bed,' said Mary Christie, looking past Lydia and the doctor. So Maryanne closed the door and thus extinguished all light except for a thin golden line below. She dropped to her hands and knees and shuffled forward into the snorts and farts of the sleeping, touching the heavy base of each berth as she passed it, counting until she reached her own.

At night, the hatches were closed and bolted from above, and the barred door was locked, and all the women except Elizabeth Duncan whom the captain took were kept inside there. There was air only from the scuttles, which you could not feel at all from the lower berths.

That night was particularly close. She was unspeakably tired. She crawled as softly as she could into the space where she lay pressed between Sarah Ward and Maria Green, a woman with a bosom so large it weighted her firmly to the mattress so she spent the nights complaining that she could not roll over. On the other side of Maria Green lay a bony and sour-smelling woman from London whose name Maryanne had heard but could not remember. The mattress felt damp and her blanket was not there.

Sarah Ward tossed and turned and abruptly threw her arms around Maryanne, pulled at her, and fell deeply asleep with her sharp cheek pressed into Maryanne's face. Maryanne lay with her nose and mouth pressed into the pillow that smelt of sea and, beneath that, vomit, and beneath that, straw, down below in the place where she did not choose to be. But it was where she was, and she put her own arms around Sarah Ward and went to sleep, until she should be needed. But she was not called upon to wet-nurse again that night.

.   .   .

'Maryanne,' whispered Sarah, poking her in the side. Maryanne rose out of sleep and sat up, but Sarah pushed her back down.

'What is wrong?' asked Maryanne.

'Hush! Speak softly!' Sarah hissed. 'I had a dream about our arrival, and I knew I must wake you. We must have a serious conversation about what we will do when we get there.'

'Should not we wait until morning?'

'No – I'll forget. We must talk now. I've heard that all the men there will come on board the ship and we'll stand before them and they'll choose from amongst us their little serving girls. I'll be all right because of my red hair and my good teeth, and I can show an ankle and smile. But you and I must remain together, and you're such a little mouse they might not even see you. So you must stand beside me when the time comes. And perhaps we can listen to what the man says – the man who chooses me – and we'll come up with something for you when he speaks. You can be a nursemaid if he tells me he has children. I wish you spoke a little rougher, a little more like me. He may hate you for sounding the same as him. He will probably want to be above you in every way. I spose that Fernsby carries it off, doesn't she? But you ain't a Fernsby. Anyway, I'll teach you to speak like a harlot, so that if we decide that's what the man wants, you can say your Oh Yes Please Sir in a sly little street voice.' Sarah Ward sighed and said, 'So that's that,' then fell asleep again. Maryanne was left to lie awake, turning this over in her head.

X

Mary Piper did not get up with the others when they were roused by the bell in the morning. The women who shared her berth leant over her and felt her skin. 'Poor little thing,' said one of them, crossing herself.

'Silly girl,' said another, crossing herself also. 'Too proud for the doctor.'

'No, it was not pride,' said the first.

'Besides, are we not allowed a little pride?' said Joan Beattie from across the room.

'Well, I suppose we are allowed it, but we might as well all now mark its consequences,' said the second woman who had spoken, and all who could see looked down at the dead body lying there, bunched up under the blanket.

Maryanne was listening, and she could see Mary Piper, although she had become distracted by her own breasts, which were fuller and heavier than they had been before. She glanced at the hospital door, but it remained closed.

There was the creak and thud of the hatch and a pair of shiny boots brought an officer down with his keys. 'What cheer is this?' he said, shaking the key in the lock, bringing the barred door open. 'Ah, a girl has died? That is a pity. Well, come up on deck and leave her there. The doctor will be down soon.' And he went away again.

Sarah Ward had been folding their blankets to take above to air, but now she flung them away from her. 'He ought to care more than that!' she cried. 'It ought to be more than a pity!' Maryanne was shushing her, afraid the officer would hear, and Sarah Ward shoved her, hard, right in her sore breasts, and she stumbled back. 'Fucking God damn them all to hell!' Sarah shouted, then screamed it again, so loud and high the words themselves became nothing but a distorted shriek, and she punched the bulkhead hard, and again, and again, until her knuckles were bloody.

'Well now,' said Maria Green, picking up the blankets. 'There is no call for that.'

.　　.　　.

The ocean was buckling in on itself, blue and grey and white, and the ship bounced them like knucklebones. Maryanne took herself off to sit by the stinking bedding. She felt sick. She was thinking of Sarah Ward, who had gone silent and sullen after her outburst below and had been taken off to prepare breakfast. Amongst the women assigned that task was the one from Cork who hated the two of them.

Joan Beattie was down below too, but in the hospital with the gentle young woman from Suffolk, washing Mary Piper's body, stitching her into her shroud. They said they did not mind it, because they had done it before.

Lydia Sculthorpe and her baby were amongst them once more. Lydia sat with her baby in one arm, her son on her lap, and she was swaying, humming. She stroked and stroked the boy's hair with her free hand.

Maryanne leant against the crate of bedding and closed her eyes. Her breasts were aching, dull and constant. She longed for Sarah Ward, who hurt her. No, that was not right. She drew her knees up and rested her forehead on them, breathing in the warm sourness of her own skirt. No, she was not longing for Sarah Ward.

She worried about her, just as she worried about Mary
Piper, which confused her, because Mary was beyond
worry now. As she worried for Astraea Pitchfork, who
surely would be needing milk again. As she worried
for herself. As she worried for her son. She put that
worry away, or tried to. She had got herself turned
about in her head, and she could not remember how
to put memories away. Water, water, everywhere,
she thought, but she was only layering words over a
memory of a peaceful little face and warm tight tiny
fingers and a sighing little chest which fluttered clear
and vivid below.

She felt a subtle change and raised her head.
Fernsby was standing above her. 'Dear,' she said, com-
panionably. 'Are you quite well?'

'Yes, thank you,' said Maryanne.

Fernsby looked down at her, evaluating. 'And how
did you find the new baby and happy mother last
night?'

'Very well,' said Maryanne.

'Her milk came,' called Lydia Sculthorpe across the
deck, unexpectedly. 'Just before I went out.' And she
resumed her swaying and humming.

'Well! I suppose that frees *you* of an obligation,'
said Fernsby to Maryanne.

'Yes,' said Maryanne, and felt tears start in her eyes. I want love, she thought, so ashamed it almost suffocated her.

Fernsby stooped to look fully into her face. 'You are a peculiar creature,' she said, and straightened once more. 'Well, good day,' she said.

But a desire came upon Maryanne to continue in her company, or anyone's really. 'What I do not know is why she would give her baby a name like Astraea,' she said. 'Plain names are better. Otherwise you draw attention.'

'Well, perhaps she is superstitious,' said Fernsby.

'But where has she got the name from? It is so odd.'

Fernsby regarded her in naked surprise. 'My dear girl! It is the name of our ship,' she said. 'How can you be ignorant of that?'

Maryanne could not answer this, could not articulate the guillotine she had let down on anything beyond the protracted moment they had together in their little wooden vessel with sea all around them, with nothing of getting on the ship, or being taken to it, or the place she had been taken from. At least the ship was contained. At least the long arms of terror and despair were tempered by the tedium of it, its dull routine, its boring indignities, its smallness. But

Fernsby would not care to know this, and so Maryanne did not even attempt it.

Fernsby said, 'It is a good name, I must say, it is the saving grace of this ship. That and the wine sherbet. Astraea was a star goddess,' she told Maryanne. 'She was the celestial virgin, daughter of Astraeus and Eos. She was a better virgin than the Virgin, who had a poor kind of virginity, never knowing the pleasure of a man but still not spared the agony of childbirth – and that must be worse, surely, a child tearing through a virgin's little body – and whose son grew to be a kind man who she had to watch tortured and hammered up on a cross for all to see. Astraea was a true virgin who was allowed to keep her body all to herself, even though she did live amongst men. She was the last of the gods, indeed, to be amongst us, to keep hoping that it was not so bad, because of her innocence, I think – all the others had abandoned us and left us to the corruption and horror of it, but she held out here on Earth for a long time. But then, in the end, even she saw the truth of it, the truth of mankind, and shot off up into the stars. And that is the story of Astraea. I think she became a constellation.'

'It is a shame she could not stay a girl,' said Maryanne.

'No, dear,' Fernsby replied. 'She was never a girl. She was always the stars, I think.' And she strolled away.

When the call to breakfast came, Maryanne sat on as the women and children lowered themselves down the hatch. She went slowly behind them all, with only the chaplain coming after her, but halfway down the ladder she realized this meant she would have little choice of seat. As she began to feel anxious about this, her bones ached. She suspected her body could not take much more of these terrible preoccupations. She did not know what she could do, and as she went timidly through the barred door, she looked over at their berth where Sarah Ward had shouted and sworn and punched her knuckles bloody. Her own hands were small and ineffectual.

The woman from Cork who hated her was watching from her seat. She was with six others; the tables held eight. This was a problem. The woman gestured at the empty seat. Maryanne looked around but her vision blurred with tears and she could see nothing with any clarity. And so she went and sat.

'Your friend Ward scalded herself badly,' the woman said, nudging Maryanne's shoulder with her own. Her face was set, her grey eyes cool. The other women at the table giggled.

There was something happening in the hospital. Maryanne thought she could hear raised voices, but she kept her head down.

'Well?' said the woman. 'Don't you care?'

'Yes, I do care,' said Maryanne, and the women laughed again. She wished they would be quiet so she could listen to the hospital.

'Do you care to know how she came to be so hurt?'

'Yes,' said Maryanne.

'Nosy little slut. It's not for you to know. But I may show you sometime,' she said, and pushed her, hard, so Maryanne had to brace. She tried to stand, but the woman gripped her arm to prevent her. 'There's nowhere,' said the woman. 'Entirely nowhere you might go.'

The memory of her own baby came again to Maryanne, quite distinct from Astraea Pitchfork. He had been so tiny and so light and yet had filled her arms and her whole body and the whole entire world, and a surge went through her and she shrugged off the woman and stood. But as she did so, there was a scream and a great clatter from behind the closed hospital door. The doctor shouted, 'Right! Enough!' and Astraea began to cry.

From within the door was opened, and at first flapped emptily, but then the doctor shouldered through, dragging Sarah Ward by the ear behind him. Her feet were bare and her bodice undone, and her body was all bandaged up underneath. She was crying, and scratching at him, and stumbling along as he pulled her. Her bonnet was off and her red hair was loose. Maryanne had never seen Sarah's hair like this, entirely unbound, rippling waist-length under the sun from the hatches below.

'What—' said the chaplain, who had been skulking off amongst the berths.

'I will be tried no more!' bellowed the doctor, and raised in his other hand a great pair of shears. There were shrieks from amongst the women. The doctor looked up and around at them and stopped, seeming to waver, then he shoved Sarah hard to the deck. She landed heavily with a sob on hands and knees and tried to crawl away, but he caught her by the hair and pulled her back.

Maryanne rushed forward, arms out. 'Sarah!' she said.

'Down, Maginn!' the doctor roared at her. She tried to fling herself past the chaplain at Sarah Ward, but he pulled her forcefully against his skinny form. Though she already knew of the hidden strength of men, still it surprised her, and she froze in his hands. Sarah Ward looked up at her, and the moment stretched: the helplessness of it as they saw one another there, Sarah injured on the floor, and Maryanne held fast.

The doctor pulled on a hank of Sarah's hair until her chin was up. Sarah was weeping, saying, 'No, no,' as if he were threatening to cut off her arms or her head instead. He wrapped the hair twice around his forearm, a red shock against his white shirtsleeve, then cut through it with his shears, close to her head. He dropped that piece and yanked her head back again with another and cut through it, sawing a little, nipping her ear. Long clumps of her hair dropped down all around her, laying themselves softly over her shoulders, her bandaged middle, her lap and hands. 'You'll mark me, sir, you'll mark me as bad,' she cried.

'Indeed,' he said.

XI

The carpenter had nailed the box upright outside their pen; it was against the bulkhead below the platform that held the great wheel. Sarah had gone limp on the sailor who pulled her along through the women. It was not Peter Rowe, and Maryanne wished it had been. The wish was not clearly defined, though perhaps she thought Peter Rowe would be gentler, or that there might be some part of Sarah glad to have his hands on her. Sarah was past crying, her eyes staring, her face streaked, her neck bone-white and fine, the lines of her skull like an egg's but bristled with patches of hair, her ears clotted with blood.

It was a brutal absurdity, the box. One narrow side of it was hinged and closed with a bar. The sailor drew this open and put Sarah inside. She sagged out, so he pushed her in again and closed and barred the door swiftly against her. There was room only for her to stand, and nothing but a narrow opening close to the top. Maryanne, standing as near as she could, against the rail of their pen, could see the tufted remains of Sarah's hair.

The other women were subdued, but they formed themselves into their customary circles. Maryanne expected the chaplain would tell her to sit down, but he left her alone. 'Sarah,' she called, but Sarah did not reply.

'It's a frightful thing,' said Joan Beattie softly, coming to her side.

'Oh, Joan!' said Maryanne. 'What happened?'

Joan stood close, putting a gentle hand on Maryanne's back. 'Well,' she said. 'You know I was down there with that young woman from Suffolk, tending to poor Mary Piper.'

'Yes,' said Maryanne.

'Sarah Ward came in with a scald all down her front, from cooking – it was boiling water, I think. And so the doctor took her off behind the screen to butter and bandage her. And that was fine. But then he had her remove her stockings and boots. And so she did. And then she went wild, Maryanne! She went entirely wild, shouting and tearing at the screen and pushing at the doctor himself, and I was trying to quiet her, you know, because the new baby was sleeping there, and Mary Piper's body was there, and the doctor was angry. But she was shouting, accusing him of interfering with her—'

'I did not think he would do that!' said Maryanne. 'I thought he found us too disgusting.'

'Well, no,' said Joan, lowering her voice and leaning even closer. 'He had said he was going to do an enema on her. And she took it very ill, telling him he was a filthy devil like all the rest of them.' Maryanne did not know what an enema was. 'She was betrayed,' said Joan. 'That's what she said – "You've betrayed me, you've betrayed me."'

'How long must she stay in there?'

'All day, they're saying.'

The chaplain came, and opened the gate, and went and stooped awkwardly by Sarah's box. He glanced around at the women watching him, and shuffled a little so his back was mostly to them. 'Ward,' he said into the narrow opening. 'Have you repented?'

Sarah made a sound.

The chaplain leant in closer, cocking an ear. 'What?' he said, then furrowed his brow and swung his head around to look at Maryanne. Then he sighed and left Sarah alone, for his breakfast was ready.

Maryanne stood at the railing, trying to think of something to say. Sarah had wanted a story back in the hospital, all those days ago, but Maryanne had disappointed her in that. She let herself remember her mother talking to her as she lay in bed, telling her how to make lace. That, too, would disappoint Sarah, she thought. 'I don't know what to say to you,' she said.

There was silence. The ship dipped and bucked, and a man shouted something from above. But then Sarah said, 'Maryanne.' It was soft but clear, and relief washed through Maryanne so strong she had to take hold of the railing. But then she knew she had to say the right thing in response, or Sarah would fall silent once more.

'That is not my name,' Maryanne said.

There was another silence, then Sarah said, 'What?'

'Maryanne is not my name,' she repeated. 'The gaol clerk wrote it down, but it is not what I told him.'

'Why?'

'He thought my real name too absurd.'

'What? So he chose you another?' Her voice was rough from crying, but she cleared her throat and added, 'Well, what *is* your name, then?'

'Marie Antoinette,' said the girl with the silly French name, and Sarah Ward laughed, once, with such loose surprise that the girl could only smile.

'That's ridiculous!' Sarah said, her voice weak but growing clearer as she spoke. 'Why – *why* would your mother name you that? Didn't Marie Antoinette wear silly wigs and get her head chopped off?'

'Yes,' said the girl Marie Antoinette. 'Yes, she got her head chopped clean off her body for wearing silly wigs and being a very stupid queen.'

'Oh my word, girl,' said Sarah from her box. 'I didn't know there was anything in this world left to surprise me.' She was silent again, and then she said, 'O God, release me! Send me truly mad!'

Maryanne glanced at the sky. 'It is nearly the middle of the day,' she said. 'You are halfway there.'

'Will you stay near me?'

'Yes, I will.' The girl turned and looked back over the women and girls and their children, all those faces beneath bonnets, anchoring themselves together there in the gaol that kept them from drowning. She sat down with her back against the railing, folding her hands in her lap. Fernsby was pacing the length of their pen, elegant as a doe. Joan Beattie and Elizabeth Duncan were sitting close, their heads bowed together.

Mary Christie was holding court over a number of women, and Maryanne could tell from the way she moved her hands that she was telling the story of the birth of the baby Astraea. She made some point, raising her hands before her, and the women laughed.

'Are you there?' asked Sarah.

'Yes, I am here.'

The woman from Cork looked over, annoyed, from amongst her own companions. And then all sound ended, not only laughter, but all their words and breathing and the sounds of the men and the ship beyond and below.

Lydia Sculthorpe, who had been drowsing, was now awake, her face glazed in horror. Maryanne felt a sort of fracturing of the air, of something occurring that could not be reconciled with what she knew to be true. Lydia and the baby in her arms were perfectly still, but the day collapsed around them, and Maryanne saw them slowly become suspended in the air. The ship and all the women fell away, and Maryanne felt herself fall away, and for a blink Lydia and her baby were simply there floating alone above the unmoving ocean, their shadow small on the surface. A little white winged thing nosed from the baby's wrappings and soared away, quick and bright.

'Oh dear,' said Joan Beattie, rising, and the world was there once more, the women and the ship and all of it, and to Maryanne it seemed none of them knew they had been dissolved at all. 'So it's finally happened. Oh, that's most terribly cruel.'

'What?' said Elizabeth Duncan.

Mary Christie creaked up and over to Lydia. She unwrapped the baby and then wrapped her back up again, but this time covering the face as well, which was as small and as blue as a duck's egg. Lydia's friends moved around her and they all became perfectly still, leaning in to her, like a flower half-closed.

The sun sank from its apex, slow behind slow clouds. Shadows crept from the women's bonnets and over their faces, and each of them, every soul, was quiet in this rare privacy. The sea sighed its great indifference, but then the sun rolled out from below clouds and rippled its light over the waves and brought from them a swell of gentle colour. The girl stood, and looked out, and saw nothing but a sweet green field going as far as the eye could see.

Acknowledgements

It is my privilege to live and write on palawa Country, which has shaped me in many deep and subtle ways. I would like to acknowledge the palawa and their great traditions of story and culture. I extend my respect to their Elders.

This novella largely arose from reading the journals of ship's surgeons on women's convict ships. I accessed scans of these online (the originals are with the UK National Archives and I live very, very far from there), but I also occasionally cross-checked my reading of some very loopy old cursive with transcriptions made by the researchers at the Female Convicts Research Centre. These transcriptions are very generously available through the Research Centre's website, free to all. I would like to acknowledge this scholarship and generosity.

I would like to thank Kelley Swain, who shared the novella prize with me and encouraged me to enter, and I would also like to thank Jane Rawson, who, with Kelley, read it before I entered it and said all sorts of encouraging things. We have an informal sort of writing group with Romy Wenzel and Melinda Briton, and I'd like to thank them too, because they're great and it's an inspiration to talk writing with them. Thank you also to the writers Belinda Lopez and Maree Spratt, because I bashed out a lot of this book during our Moderate-Commitment Writing Club pomodoro-inspired Zoom sessions.

Thank you to Neil, Damian and Lamorna at Weatherglass Books, who chose my manuscript to be shortlisted, and who are so wonderful to work with. Thank you to Sarah Terry for her generous and expert editor's eye. And an enormous thank you to Ali Smith, for selecting Astraea to be published. The reason I entered the prize at all, even though I had no novella ready and only a couple of months before the deadline, was because Ali was the judge.

I also need to thank my family. My husband, Matthew, who loves and supports me (generally, and also in my writing), and my children, even though they would honestly prefer it if I didn't spend any time at all writing. They begrudgingly allow it, and I'm grateful. My brothers, Hugh, Will and Samuel, and Will I'm sorry I asked you to read this when you had a newborn. Please don't read the ending.

ASTRAEA

KATE KRUIMINK

First published in 2024
by Weatherglass Books

A CIP record for this book is published by the British Library

ISBN: 9781739570767

Cover design: Luke Bird
Typesetting: James Tookey

Printed in the U.K. by TJ Books, Padstow

www.weatherglassbooks.com

Weatherglass
Books